ISBN-13: 978-1-84646-123-1
ISBN-10: 1-8464-6123-5

Manufactured in Italy

The Costume Ball

It was the day of the Costume Ball and Angelina hadn't been invited. "If you're going as a queen and Dad's going as a king, it makes sense that I go as a princess!" she said to Mrs Mouseling.

'I'm sorry Angelina," said Mrs Mouseling patiently. "The ball is for grown-ups, not little mouselings!"

"Everyone should be allowed to go to the ball," complained Angelina to Alice later. Her friend emerged from the dressing-up box wearing a hat and a dress that was far too big for her.

Alice danced until she tripped over the hem and fell on top of Angelina. "Sorry!" she giggled. "You could fit us both in this dress!"
"Yes . . ." said Angelina thoughtfully.

It was almost time for the Costume Ball to begin and Mrs Mouseling looked beautiful.

"Mrs Hodgepodge will be here to babysit any minute," she said.

"Oh, no!" groaned Angelina. "Last time she kept me awake all night with her horrible snoring!"

"I hope she doesn't bring her cabbage jelly," whispered Alice.

Mr Mouseling came into the room
dressed like a giant bee instead of a king.
"Mix up at the costume shop!" he
explained, as Angelina and Alice giggled.

Just then Mrs Hodgepodge arrived.
"Good night you two," said Mrs
Mouseling as she swept out of the door
on Mr Mouseling's arm.
"Be good for Mrs Hodgepodge!"

After a horrible dinner of cabbage jelly,
Angelina and Alice ran upstairs.
"I wish we were at the ball," sighed
Angelina. "Would you care to dance?"
"I'd love to," smiled Alice.

Downstairs Mrs Hodgepodge had fallen
asleep and was beginning to snore
loudly. Angelina was trying to listen to
the beautiful music drifting through the
window from the Ball.

"Right. Come on Alice!" exclaimed
Angelina, as she began rummaging
through the dressing-up box.
"Come on where?" asked Alice.
"To the Costume Ball of course!"

"But what about Mrs Hodgepodge?"
whispered Alice.
"She'll be asleep for hours!" replied
Angelina, tossing a hat over to Alice.

As Angelina and Alice entered the hall,
they gasped.
"Wow! Look Alice! It's wonderful!"
smiled Angelina. From within their
disguise, the two mouselings looked
around them. Angelina wobbled on
Alice's shoulders as they tottered
towards a table piled with delicious
things to eat.
"All that fooood!" cried Alice.

"Careful Alice!" whispered Angelina as
Alice grabbed a cheese ball.
"Such a wonderful party, don't you
agree, my dear?" asked a familiar voice.

It was Miss Lilly!
"Err yes, Miss . . . miss . . . absolutely
unmissable!" stuttered Angelina in her
most grown-up voice.

Luckily, just then Dr Tuttle appeared.
"I was wondering if you'd care to
dance?" he asked Miss Lilly.
"It would be a pleasure, darlink!" she
replied as she took his paw.
"See you later for the Whiskers Reel!"
said Miss Lilly as she disappeared.
"I wish someone would ask me to
dance," said Angelina glumly as she
watched them make their way onto the
crowded dance floor.

Back at the Mouseling's cottage, Mrs
Hodgepodge woke up when she felt a
draught. "It's coming from Angelina's
room," she muttered as she went to
investigate. The window was wide open.

At the ball, Angelina was desperate to
dance when a voice announced, "Take
your positions for the Whiskers Reel!"
"Come on Alice!" she whispered.
Everyone lined up and the music started.

As they danced, Angelina began to lose her balance on Alice's shoulders. She wobbled, and bumped into her father, but luckily he didn't recognise her. Then they stumbled into the table, and cheese balls flew everywhere as the two mouselings landed in a sticky heap.

Just at that moment, Mrs Hodgepodge threw open the doors of the hall.

"There they are, those naughty little runaways!" she cried.
"Angelina!" gasped Mr and Mrs Mouseling.

Everyone stared at the two mouselings as they sat on the floor, surrounded by cheese balls and trying hard not to cry.

Now they were in real trouble.

Angelina and Alice were up early the next morning. There was a great deal of mess to be cleared up in the hall.

"My back's aching! This is such hard work!" groaned Alice, mopping the floor. "I'm so tired! Perhaps going to the ball wasn't such a good idea," sighed Angelina as she scrubbed away.

The door opened and Mrs Mouseling
came in with Mrs Hodgepodge.
"We've brought you something to eat!"
said Angelina's mother, smiling.

Angelina and Alice took huge bites from
the delicious looking sandwiches.

"Oh, no!" they groaned.
"Cabbage jelly!"